Buttercup Mystery

Misty ^{'s} Inn

Buttercup Mystery

By Kristin Earhart

Illustrated by Serena Geddes

ALADDIN
New York London Toronto Sydney New Delhi

ALADDIN

An imprint of Simon & Schuster Children's Publishing Division

1230 Avenue of the Americas, New York, NY 10020

First Aladdin hardcover edition June 2015

Text copyright © 2015 by The Estate of Marguerite Henry

Illustrations copyright © 2015 by Serena Geddes

Also available in an Aladdin paperback edition.

For information about special discounts for bulk purchases, please contact Simon & Schuster Special Sales at 1-866-506-1949 or business@simonandschuster.com.

The Simon & Schuster Speakers Bureau can bring authors to your live event. For more information or to book an event contact the Simon & Schuster Speakers Bureau at 1-866-248-3049 or visit our website at www.simonspeakers.com.

Designed by Laura Lyn DiSiena

The text of this book was set in Century Expanded.

Manufactured in the United States of America 0515 FFG

10 9 8 7 6 5 4 3 2 1

Library of Congress Control Number 2015937387

ISBN 978-1-4814-1417-3 (hc)

ISBN 978-1-4814-1416-6 (pbk)

ISBN 978-1-4814-1418-0 (eBook)

To Olivia, Sophie, and Riley Kate

Buttercup Mystery

Chapter 1

"HEY, YOU GUYS IN THERE?"

Willa looked at her brother, Ben. "It's Chipper," she whispered. "You want to do it?"

Ben looked at the bucket above the door. The bucket was half full of water. A string was tied to its handle. The string was in Ben's hand. He had been using it to play with New Cat.

Ben chewed his lip. Chipper Starling was

his new best friend. Ben and Willa had lived on Chincoteague Island for only a few weeks. Ben thought for a few seconds and nodded at Willa.

"Yeah, we're here, Chipper. Come on in." Willa was at the back of the barn, out of the way.

As soon as Chipper poked his head in the tall double doors, Ben gave a yank. It could not have worked better. The water fell on Chipper, the bucket fell on the ground, and laughter filled the air.

"Got you back," Ben said.

"That was a good one." Chipper wrung out his shirt. New Cat, who also got wet, was licking the unwanted water from her fur.

"Nice job!" Willa gave Ben a high five. Chipper did the same.

Willa smiled when she saw the two boys

laughing. She was glad her brother had found a friend who shared his sense of humor. Even better, Chipper had a sister. His sister was the same age as Willa, and she loved horses and other animals. How lucky could Willa get?

It was funny, because Willa had not felt lucky when they had first moved. She had missed Chicago and her friends. She had not known if Chincoteague, with all its sand and salty air, could be home.

Even though their mom had grown up on the island, Willa and Ben had not spent much time in the little beach town. It was a big change for the whole family. They had left the city and a small apartment and now lived in a big Victorian house with three stories and a wraparound porch.

"You guys should come over to our place," Chipper said. A drip of water streamed from his forehead down his cheek. "Sarah wants to show you something, Willa. She sent me to tell you especially."

"Really? What is it?"

"I'm not allowed to tell." Chipper shrugged. "She was too excited, but she's stuck at home with Bess."

Bess was Sarah and Chipper's little sister. They had to watch her sometimes while their mom worked. Willa rested the broom in the corner. "You guys go ahead. I'll tell Mom and Dad." As she walked to the house, Willa tried to figure out what could be so exciting. Why wouldn't Sarah at least offer a hint? Willa could think of only one thing that was *that* exciting to her.

Willa watched her brother and Chipper shuffle down the drive, kicking up dust and sand on their way. She skipped up the porch steps and wiped the dirt off her freckled knees. "Mom, Dad?" she called. "I'm going over to Sarah's!" She headed down the hallway and, no surprise, found them both in the kitchen. Their old kitchen had room for only one person at a time, but this kitchen was four times that size. It needed to be. It would have to feed a lot more people when the family's bed-and-breakfast opened.

The Dunlaps had never run a hotel—or a restaurant—before. But Ben and Willa's dad had been a chef for years, and their mom liked a challenge. The family had agreed on Misty Inn as a name. Misty was a famous pony that had lived on Chincoteague long ago.

Willa glanced around the kitchen. It looked like Dad was already cooking for a whole hotel. Bowls of tomatoes, jars of spices, and mounds of chopped peppers covered the counter. "It's kind of early to be making dinner, isn't it?" Willa asked.

"He's trying out chili recipes," Mom said as Dad dumped some red powder into a steaming pot.

"I'm entering the Greater Chincoteague Chili Cook-Off," Dad explained. "And I plan to win it." He took a tiny taste from a large wooden spoon. "This is my second batch today."

Willa looked at the large clock above the stove. It wasn't even ten in the morning. "So, can we go to the Starlings'?" she asked. "Sarah has something to show me."

"Of course," Mom said. She smiled at Willa

from the other side of the laptop. "I'm just trying to find furniture for the guest bedrooms
today. Not very exciting."

Even though Mom said that, Willa knew her
mom loved that kind of stuff. In the new house,
Willa and Ben got their own bedrooms. Their
parents would share one, and then there were
three left over. The extra rooms would be for
guests, and Mom wanted the beds and dressers
to look old and stately.

Willa knew these things were fun for her parents. But she couldn't stay there another second. A surprise was waiting for her at the Starlings' house. But what?

"Wow, another horse?" Willa couldn't believe it. The Starlings already had one horse in their pasture, along with a couple of goats. Of course, a horse had been the one thing that Willa had thought of when Chipper said "exciting." Willa couldn't even imagine having one horse in her backyard, let alone two.

"Her name is Buttercup," Sarah said, rubbing the new horse's velvety muzzle. "Once she's settled in, Dad will use her for the pony swim and all that."

Sarah's dad was one of the island's saltwater

cowboys, which meant that he had the special job of helping with the roundups of the wild ponies on nearby Assateague.

From Chincoteague, Assateague looked like a little wisp of land before the great big open ocean. The small island was the home of two herds of wild ponies—ponies whose ancestors had escaped a stormy shipwreck hundreds of years before. They'd been taking care of themselves ever since.

Thinking about the wild ponies reminded Willa of Starbuck, the beautiful buckskin pony at her grandparents' nearby farm. Willa and Ben's grandma was a vet and had once run an animal rescue center on the island. Recently, a neighbor had left Starbuck at Miller Farm because the pony's owner could no longer care for her.

Willa and Ben were more than happy to look after Starbuck, but Grandma Edna felt that healthy animals did not need to be there. They needed to find new homes—forever homes.

"If your dad is going to use Buttercup for roundups, what about Sweetums?" Willa asked. She reached out to give the older horse a steady pat on his shiny black coat.

"That's the best part," Sarah said. "Dad knows how much I love Sweetums, so he's going to let me ride him more. He might even let me ride Sweetums in the carnival parade."

"No way!" Willa said. Chincoteague's Summer Extravaganza had rides, game booths, and tons of tasty food. The parade was on a Saturday morning and went straight through the town. It was for the local horses and pets, as well as some old cars and unicycles. Willa and Ben had heard all about the silly costumes people wore. It sounded like their kind of fun.

"Well, Dad said I have to earn it," Sarah explained. "He'll make me do lots of chores. I'll probably have to muck stalls and stack hay. It might not be worth it."

Willa nodded. She didn't care how much manure she had to shovel. She'd clean out a hundred stalls if she could ride a horse in that parade.

Chapter 2

THE NEXT AFTERNOON WILLA, SARAH, AND Sarah's little sister, Bess, were sitting in the deep grass right next to the Starlings' pasture.

Sarah was listing all the things she had to do before she could ride in the parade. "And I also have to babysit Bess more," she complained.

As cute as Bess was, Willa knew she could

be a handful. "She's kind of quiet today," Willa commented.

"Yeah. Ever since we got Buttercup, all she wants to do is feed her," Sarah replied.

"She likes how, every once in a while, Buttercup just takes off. She'll gallop across the field and throw in a couple of bucks here and there. Bess cracks up every time. She loves it."

"Pretty horsey," Bess whispered as she picked clover stems and made a bouquet. "Pretty Buttercup."

Buttercup was a tall, slender horse with a glistening chestnut coat. She had a small star between her warm eyes. But every once in a while, those eyes sparkled with real mischief.

Willa wondered how the horse got her name. She looked nothing like the small yellow flower that grew like a weed in the summertime.

"Does she like to eat buttercups?" Willa thought out loud.

"I doubt it. They taste horrible," Sarah said. "See how they're all over the pasture? They're too bitter, so no one eats them. Not even the goats."

Willa laughed out loud.

Even though they'd

15

known the other family only a month, she and Ben had already seen the Starlings' goats eat a gym shoe, a juice box, and one of Bess's dirty diapers. Actually, Mrs. Starling had rescued the diaper just in time, but not the shoe. When Chipper finally wrestled it from Kirby, just a shoelace was left.

"At least the horses keep her in one place," Willa said, nodding at Bess.

"No joke," Sarah agreed. "Dad calls her Houdini in pigtails." Willa wasn't surprised that they compared Bess to the famous magician. She was a real escape artist. "Chipper says we should get some kind of tracking device for her."

Just then Willa heard Ben's laughter. It was getting closer.

"Stop him!" Chipper called out. "He's out of control!" The boys were chasing a puppy.

Sarah jumped up. "Amos!" she cried.

Willa was on her feet in seconds too. All four kids raced after the black-and-white pup with the bright pink tongue. Amos zigged and zagged. The kids' fingers groped and grabbed, but no one could catch him. Finally he ran under the pasture fence and stopped, panting, next to Buttercup.

The horse turned her big head and snuffled at the puppy. Amos sniffed back, then licked the horse's muzzle.

"That's so cute!" Willa squealed.

"They always do that," Chipper insisted, resting his hands on his knees while he caught his breath.

"Always? *Really?* We just got Buttercup yesterday," Sarah pointed out.

"But I've seen Amos lick her like that, like, four times."

"Well, they'd better not get too attached," Sarah warned. "We have to start giving the puppies away soon."

Amos was one of seven puppies. The Starlings' dog, Marnie, had had puppies earlier that summer.

"Have you decided which one you're going to keep?" Ben asked.

"I like Amos," Chipper said. "He's fun, but Mom wants someone to adopt him."

"He'd be too much work," Sarah explained. "I really like Rice Cake and Jubilee. I think they'd be happy getting to stay with Marnie, but Dad says we can only keep one."

It seemed like everyone on Chincoteague had pets to spare, except Willa and Ben. Of course, they did have New Cat, but she wasn't really a pet. New Cat's job was to keep the mice away, and she was very good at it. Yes, she was soft and sweet, but she was a homebody. She didn't do tricks or go on adventures with Ben and Willa.

"Rice Cake and Jubilee might want to stay with their mom, but Amos looks like he's more attached to Buttercup," Ben observed. The puppy was playfully running loops around the tall mare. Buttercup did her best to ignore him. When he stopped and yipped, Buttercup snorted and trotted to the other side of the pasture. Amos followed her.

"He's trying to herd Buttercup," Chipper announced with a laugh.

"Buttercup!" Bess cried, holding out a giant bouquet of fresh clover. "Buttercup, come back! Buttercup!"

"Bess, leave her alone. Buttercup needs to get settled so I can ride Sweetums in the parade." Sarah stood up and grabbed her little sister by the hand, trying to tug her away. "Maybe we should take her down to the dock," Sarah suggested, looking at her brother.

"Ben and I have to get going," Willa said. "Our grandparents should be back by now."

"Do you have to go?" Sarah said. It now seemed funny to Willa that she and Sarah had not become friends as soon as they met. . . . At first, Willa thought Sarah was bossy and rude. That seemed so long ago!

"They're expecting us," Willa said, not wanting to hurt Sarah's feelings. Besides, it was the truth. At least, it was part of the truth. The whole truth was that Willa didn't want to spend the whole day fussing over Buttercup, Sweetums, and Bess. She wanted to see Starbuck, who was the most wonderful pony Willa had ever known.

"Yeah," Ben agreed. "They'll have stuff for us to do." Willa smiled at her brother. He was anxious to see Starbuck too.

♥

Starbuck greeted them with a happy whinny. "I think she hears the rattle of our bikes," Ben said as they propped the kickstands into place. "She just calls out. She doesn't even lift her head all the way to make sure it's us."

Grandma Edna looked up from her sweeping. "Animals have a sixth sense," she said. "For weather, for food, for danger. They rely on their instincts." She grabbed a long lead and headed for the paddock gate. "That mare's got good instincts. She's always been certain about you two."

Willa smiled. Grandma Edna was no-nonsense. She gave compliments only when she really meant them.

When Starbuck had first arrived, she'd been

hurt. The pony had limped because her leg was sore. Being a vet, Grandma Edna had known how to treat it. Willa and Ben had helped, wrapping the leg and keeping Starbuck company in the stall. But they'd never been allowed to ride her. Not yet.

"We've got to get this pony some exercise," Grandma said. "She has to be in shape if we're going to find her a new home."

Ben and Willa let out matching sighs. Neither could think about Starbuck going to another home—unless it was theirs.

"I'm going to play with Bee Bee Bun," Ben announced. Bee Bee Bun was an angora rabbit that was missing half an ear but had all his personality.

"That's good," Grandma said. "You can help

Clifton clean his hutch." Ben nodded. Clifton was a high school boy who helped around the barn. Clifton wanted to be a vet, and Ben thought that was super cool.

Willa and Grandma stood in the center of the paddock. Starbuck circled them on the long lead. "Give her a click. Get her to trot," Grandma directed.

Willa clicked her tongue, and the pony sped up. "Well, look at that," Grandma murmured. "She can move." The pony had a long, even stride.

Willa thought Starbuck looked beautiful. She wondered what it would be like to ride the pony. "Sarah might get to ride in the carnival parade," Willa said, surprising herself. She hadn't planned on telling Grandma.

"Is that so?" Grandma replied.

"The Starlings got a new horse," Willa explained. "So Sarah would ride Sweetums."

"Sweetums is a mighty fine horse," Grandma said. "But that parade is a mess. I wouldn't trust most horses with such a young rider. Someone's likely to get hurt."

Willa felt a knot in her belly. Was Grandma right?

"Hi, Mrs. Miller!" a voice rang out. Willa found its owner right away—a girl with long braids pulled into a low, thick ponytail. Her smile stretched all the way across her face.

"My parents sent me for Clifton." Before Grandma could respond, the girl spoke again. "You must be Willa! I'm Lena. I'm so excited to finally meet you! Sarah told me all about you in her letters. I've been away at piano camp, but now I'm back and we'll hang out. You, me, and Sarah will be like the three musketeers!"

"Okay," Willa said softly.

"Hey, sis." Clifton came up behind her and tugged on one of her many braids. "I heard you a mile away. We should go."

With that, Clifton picked up Lena, plopped her on his bike seat, and put a helmet on her head.

"Willa! Come to the ice-cream parlor at three tomorrow," Lena instructed. "It's my birthday."

Grandma chuckled to herself. "That girl's got ten words for every one from her brother."

Willa watched as they rode away. Willa's friendship with Sarah had been very slow to start, but Lena was great gangbusters.

Chapter 3

THE NEXT DAY, SARAH PICKED UP WILLA FOR the party. Chipper and Ben were going too. "Lena's lots of fun," Sarah said, "except she doesn't like horses."

"That's weird," Willa said before she could stop herself. They were walking to Lena's party at Four Corners, taking a shortcut on a side street.

"She doesn't hate them or anything," Sarah replied. "But her parents won't let her ride. They're worried she'll fall off and get hurt. Then she couldn't play piano."

"Not if she broke her leg," Chipper said. "She could still play then."

"You should tell her parents," Sarah said. "Maybe they'll change their minds." Chipper and Ben both rolled their eyes. Big sisters.

Grandma Edna had mentioned that Lena was a good musician. Sarah had said that Lena was not allowed to play until she had practiced piano for an hour each day. Willa had known kids like that back in Chicago.

It felt funny, going to the birthday party of someone she barely knew. Luckily, Willa and Ben were going in on Sarah and Chipper's gift for Lena. "It's a huge boxed set of mystery books," Sarah had explained. "Lena loves detective stories and spooky stuff."

Willa would never have guessed that! She would have had no clue if she had had to choose a gift for Lena.

"Hey! Hey!"

Willa spotted Lena in the middle of the outside courtyard, surrounded by bunches of silver balloons. Clifton was there, along with some other kids Willa and Sarah's age.

"Check it out," Lena said, rushing up to the fence. She pointed to a turquoise bike. It wasn't an ordinary bike. It was raised up on a stand so it wouldn't go anywhere. Plus, it had extra gears that were attached to a wooden bucket. "We're going to ride this bike and

make the energy to churn the ice cream."

Willa had never seen anything like it. "We can really make that much energy? On a bike?"

Lena nodded. "Whatever we make I get to take home."

"I'm next!" yelled Chipper. He rushed forward and climbed through the fence's wooden rails.

"Then me!" Ben said, right on Chipper's heels. They lined up next to the bike.

Willa bit her lip. At least Ben wasn't worried about fitting in.

Sarah grabbed her hand. Willa ducked under the fence behind her friend. Sarah was great. She introduced her to all the other kids. Then Lena motioned for them to sit down with her at the center picnic table.

"This is a big party," Willa said.

"I know," Lena admitted. "My mom's on the PTA and she works at the museum, so I have to invite *everyone*." She pushed her beaded braids over her shoulder. "But even if it were a small party, I would have invited you, Willa."

Willa smiled, but she didn't know what to say to the birthday girl.

"Hey, Sarah," a kid called from the line by the bike. "Bet I can make more energy than you." Sarah glanced over her shoulder but then turned back around. "Time me," he yelled. "I can go five minutes."

"I don't think so," Sarah answered, not even making eye contact with the boy. As soon as he had taken his place on the bike, Sarah glared at Lena. "Yick," she whispered. "Did you have to invite Jasper Langely?" Willa had never seen

Sarah look so disgusted, not even when Sarah stepped in their barn cat's throw-up—in her bare feet.

Lena leaned forward as if the three girls were sharing the juiciest secret. "Jasper's not that bad. My mom always works with his mom at the carnival." Willa glanced at the boy again. In the midday sun, she could see sweat popping up where his pale blond hair parted. He scowled as his legs whizzed around on the pedals.

Sarah turned to Willa. "He has been in my class every year. He's pretty smart, but he always wants to bet on who will get the best grade on a test. It's annoying."

"You should take that bet," Lena suggested. "You always get the highest score."

"Nope," Sarah said, smoothing the creases

from her skirt. "If I say yes once, he'll bug me all the time. He will bet on anything!"

A few minutes later Jasper called to Sarah again. "I bet I've churned enough ice cream for three giant sundaes."

"Good!" Lena responded. "That's enough for Sarah, Willa, and me. Thanks."

"Come on, Sarah," Jasper begged. "Take a turn."

"No," Sarah replied. "I'm saving my energy for barn chores so I can ride in the carnival parade."

"No way!" Jasper exclaimed, climbing off the bike. "How come you get to ride? You haven't before."

"Neither have you." Sarah turned to face Jasper. After a pause, she added, "My dad got a new horse, so he's going to let me ride Sweetums."

"That old nag? I'm riding my dad's horse, Wrangler."

"Sweetums isn't old," Willa said, defending Sarah's favorite.

"Like you know anything about horses," Jasper said, looking Willa up and down. "You aren't even from Chincoteague."

Willa felt a knot in her stomach. How could he say that?

Jasper turned back to Sarah. "There's no way you'll get to ride."

"Oh, yeah?" Sarah questioned.

"Yeah. You wanna bet?"

"Sure."

It wasn't long before they agreed on the

terms of the bet. All Sarah had to do was ride in the parade, and she would win. If she didn't get to ride, she would lose. The loser had to buy the winner the biggest ice-cream sundae on the Four Corners menu.

"It's a deal." Jasper and Sarah shook hands.

"Whoa, the biggest sundae? That's the one with the homemade brownie, the caramel, and the fudge," Lena pointed out.

"I know," Sarah said. "It's my favorite. I *have* to win. And prove that Jasper Langely doesn't know everything!"

Chapter 4

THE DAY AFTER THE PARTY, WILLA HAD
an idea. It was a great idea. If Sarah was
doing chores to be in the parade, maybe she
could too. More than anything, Willa would
love to ride Starbuck in the parade. But that
was a long shot. She hadn't even been able to
ride Starbuck at Miller Farm yet. Still, Willa
was willing to do lots of chores. She wanted

Grandma to see how responsible she could be.

"I need to go to Miller Farm," Willa announced at breakfast. "I'm going to ask Grandma Edna if I can have some regular chores."

"That's a great idea," Mom said between sips of coffee. "Why don't you start here first? I'll give you chores."

Willa's shoulders drooped. "What kind of chores?"

"Any kind. All kinds!" Mom sounded excited. "When the inn opens up, this place is going to have to run like clockwork. Your dad and I will need your help."

Hearing this, Willa had a hard time swallowing her toast. Ben had a hard time hiding a smirk, until Mom spoke again. "Ben, you'll need some chores of your own." His smirk disappeared.

After breakfast, the brother and sister met in Willa's room. Willa had a clipboard. "We have to make a list of chores. Chores we can do, so the house runs like clockwork," Willa said.

"Our house will never run like clockwork. Unless the clock is broken," Ben said.

It was a joke, but it was also true. The Dunlaps had bad habits. They ran late. Their dirty laundry piles grew to the size of mountains. Mail and homework stacks were lopsided towers on the dinner table.

"Why did you have to volunteer us for chores?" Ben asked.

"I wanted to do chores at the farm, so I can ride in the parade," Willa explained. "Like Sarah."

"You think Mom would let you?" Ben asked.

"Yeah. But Grandma is going to be a harder sell." Willa had heard her dad use that phrase. It meant that it wasn't easy to convince someone. It would be hard to sell them on your idea. Grandma Edna might be the hardest sell of all time.

"Yeah, you're right. But riding in the parade would be fun," admitted Ben. "We'd be real Chincoteague kids then."

Willa looked at Ben. He had a faraway look in his eyes. Did he want to ride in the parade too?

"Let's start in the bathroom," Willa said. "First off, towels should not be on the floor. We have a towel rack for that."

Ben rolled his eyes. "The towels always slip off," he complained.

"Then use the hook on the back of the door,"

Willa suggested as she filled out her chore chart. "Let's look at your room."

They came up with a good list together.

Throw dirty clothes in the laundry basket.

Make beds.

Park bikes in the barn.

Sweep decks.

Water flowers.

"I also told Mom we'd put our dirty dishes in the sink and take turns setting the table," Willa said after they had taken a full tour of the house.

"I told her we'd feed New Cat," Ben told his sister.

"That seems like a good start," Willa stated, hoping they'd still have time for chores at Miller Farm.

"I also said we'd look after Mrs. Cornett's chickens," Ben added, "but only when they get in our yard." Their neighbor had a lot of chickens. Some of the chickens liked to visit the Dunlaps' backyard. The hens pecked in the grass and at the orange flowers on the fence. Ben really liked the chickens.

"Okay," murmured Willa. "Let's not volunteer for anything else, or we won't have any time left."

"Okay," agreed Ben. The two went to find Mom.

"This will be so helpful," Mom said as she reviewed the checklist. "You can get started now. Once you're done, you can go to Sarah and Chipper's or the farm. Grandma said she wants you there first thing tomorrow. She said it's going to be a big day."

Willa's mind leaped at the news. A big day? They were going to get to ride Starbuck. She was sure of it! She really wanted to tell Sarah, but she didn't want to jinx it. She closed her eyes and wished she were right.

♥

"Buttercup is acting weird," Sarah said when Willa arrived at the Starlings'. "She's not as peppy as when she showed up."

"Maybe she was just showing off at first," Chipper said. "Maybe she's not a peppy pony at all."

Sarah shook her head.

"Buttercup," Bess yodeled, waving a fistful of grass and clover. "Flowers for Buttercup!" Bess thrust them through the fence.

The tall chestnut horse dragged her hooves

over to Bess. She reached out her long, neck and nibbled at the stems in Bess's hand.

"Dad just looked at her this morning and sighed," Sarah said. "What if he decides not to ride Buttercup in the parade?"

Willa knew exactly what Sarah was thinking. Of course she was concerned about the new horse, but it was more than that. If Mr. Starling didn't ride Buttercup in the parade, Sarah couldn't ride Sweetums. If Sarah didn't ride Sweetums, Sarah would lose the bet with Jasper.

Chapter 5

THE NEXT MORNING, WILLA AND BEN RODE THEIR bikes to their grandparents' place in near silence. They were both thinking of the same thing.

"You can go first," Willa said. They propped their bikes against the far side of the farmhouse and then hurried to the barn.

"How come you're letting me go?" Ben asked.

"Can't I do something nice?" responded Willa. She tried to sound offended, but Ben had a right to be suspicious. Willa did want to get on Starbuck as soon as she could. However, she also had a plan. She suspected she would get a longer turn if she went second.

"Doesn't she look lovely?" Grandma Edna asked. She had already tacked up Starbuck. A fluffy white pad rested under the saddle on her back. The leather bridle brought out the deep chocolate brown of her eyes and mane. "I can tell by the look on your faces that your mom already told you."

"She just said it was a big day," replied Willa.

"Well, it is," Grandma declared. "You'll be riding Starbuck."

The three of them headed out to the small paddock together. There, the grassy ground was softer. It would be easier on Starbuck's newly healed leg.

The normally calm pony's ears twitched in every direction, and she gave a quick snort. "She's ready," Grandma Edna said, pushing a helmet into Ben's hands. "Are you?"

"I think so," Ben mumbled.

"You can't be wishy-washy with horses, Ben," Grandma Edna insisted. "Horses need a sure hand." Ben knew that tone; it was just like Willa's. He tried to remember if Grandma Edna was also a big sister.

"I know," Ben declared. "I am ready." He may not have had all the riding lessons Willa had back in Chicago, but he loved Starbuck every bit as much. He put his left foot in the stirrup and pulled himself up.

"There you go," Grandma said. She gave Starbuck a slap on the rump, and the pony moved to the far end of the lead line. Grandma stood in the middle, and Starbuck walked around her.

"How about a trot?" Grandma Edna clicked her tongue, and Starbuck picked up her pace.

It was fun. Ben couldn't believe he was riding Starbuck. He and Willa had waited so long! He had gone around the small circle several times before he started feeling woozy.

"Grandma, I think he's getting dizzy," Willa warned.

"No, I'm not," Ben protested, but his head churned like a blender. He felt like he might slide right out of the saddle.

"He looks good," said Grandma, full of pride.

Ben felt his body start to tilt.

"Whoa, that's enough, Ben." Grandma Edna stopped the merry-go-round just in time. Ben still felt woozy on the ground. He heard Willa giggle as he stumbled off toward the barn.

"Nice and easy," Grandma called out to Willa, who was rushing toward Starbuck. Dust rose up from under her boots. Her excitement was bubbling and bursting in every muscle. She had to force herself to slow down to a walk.

"You need to be steady, Willa. You never want to startle a horse. They'll suspect danger."

Willa knew this. She knew that in the wild horses had to be alert. They were always on the lookout. But it was hard to be "nice and easy" when she was so close!

She took a deep breath as she grabbed the saddle. She hoisted herself up. Her toes searched for the stirrups, and she pushed her weight into her heels.

Willa could hardly believe it. She ran her hand along the pony's neck. Starbuck was soft and warm and wonderful.

"Ask her to walk on," Grandma instructed.

As soon as Willa squeezed her legs around Starbuck's belly, the pony responded.

"And trot."

Willa clicked her tongue, and Starbuck sprang ahead.

Willa's rear popped out of the saddle with each bouncy step. Even though the lead line was attached to the pony's bridle, it was still fun. Starbuck had a happy stride.

In no time, Grandma had them turn around. "Want to try it without the lead, steering on your own?" she asked.

"Yes!"

Grandma started to pull them in.

"Edna, phone!" Grandpa's yell came from the house.

"Just a minute!" Grandma called back as she unclipped the lead from the bridle. "Hold tight," she said, giving Starbuck a pat. "I'll be right back."

Starbuck stamped her foot, so Willa let the pony walk in the paddock. It was going so well, Willa wondered if they might get to try to canter. Willa liked to canter most of all. What if Starbuck could jump? How soon would they get to try that?

The door slammed. Grandma marched out, arms swinging at her sides.

"That'll be it for today," she said.

"But—" Willa started to say when Grandma clutched at the bridle, and Starbuck stopped.

"Sorry to cut it short, sweetie." Grandma's voice had turned soft, but her words were still hurried. "The Starlings' new horse is sick, real sick, and you have to come with me."

Willa's heart fell to her foot as she lowered herself to the dusty ground. Sure, she was disappointed at not being able to keep riding, but her thoughts had now leaped to Sarah . . . and to Buttercup.

Chapter 6

WHEN GRANDMA EDNA, WILLA, AND BEN arrived, everyone at the Starlings' place was quiet. Even Lena, who had come over to try to cheer up Sarah, did not smile.

"What seems to be the problem?" Grandma Edna asked, still a dozen steps away from the pasture gate.

Mr. Starling unlatched the lock to open it for

her. "Buttercup's been lazy for the past couple of days," he explained. "It was quite a change. She was a real spark plug when she first got here."

Willa remembered the horse playing with Amos, the mischievous puppy. Whenever Amos nipped at her leg, she had run away across the field. She had seemed very lively—and hungry for clover and grass.

Now Buttercup looked weary. Her head drooped. She hardly twitched an ear when Grandma approached. Mr. Starling held Buttercup's halter and talked softly while Grandma took a good, long look.

She sighed and ran her hands over the horse's legs. After rummaging in her kit, she pulled out a stethoscope and pressed

it to the horse's belly. Next, she moved to Buttercup's head.

"There's something not right," Grandma agreed. "Her eyes are dull. Her lips are swollen. Tender gums." Wearing thin gloves, Grandma felt all around Buttercup's mouth. "What's she been eating?"

Mr. Starling went on to explain that Buttercup had been eating all the same things as Sweetums: same hay, same grain, same grass. "They got along so well, they've been in the same field from the start. I don't get why Buttercup is sick but Sweetums is fine. I don't think it's the food."

Grandma made her way to the center of the pasture and kneeled down. Willa wondered, *What is she doing?* She had a twig and

was poking in a pile of something. *Yuck! Horse manure!*

"Things look okay here," Grandma said. "Not too hard or too runny. You should watch for any changes. And I'd like to check your bag of grain, just in case," Grandma said. "There's also the chance that Buttercup got hold of something poisonous. I'm sure you know that buttercups are toxic." Grandma pointed to the tall, straggly plants in the pasture, each with clusters of tiny yellow flowers at the top.

Mr. Starling nodded. "Horses don't touch it. It's too bitter."

Grandma walked over to the nearest buttercup plant and tugged. The tough stem came out roots and all. "Let's just make sure," she said as she walked back and offered Buttercup the

delicate flowers. Buttercup gave a lazy sniff
and turned away.

"I'll think on it, Lloyd. The horse is not herself, but she's not too bad off." She watched
Buttercup as she loaded up her vet kit. "We'd
best keep an eye on her. I can run some tests if
she doesn't improve." The two adults headed to
the barn to look at the grain. Bess was behind
them, picking clover as she went.

"Where are the puppies?" Ben asked. Willa

rolled her eyes. Didn't he care about Buttercup
at all?

"They're with Marnie," Chipper said. "Amos
won't leave Buttercup alone, so Dad made us
put them all in the outdoor pen, at least until
the vet is gone. Your grandma, I mean."

"Let's go get them," Ben said, taking off.

The girls didn't want to leave Buttercup.

As soon as the boys were gone, Sarah
blurted out, "I feel so bad. I keep thinking
about the parade instead of worrying about
Buttercup."

"My daddy always tells me worrying won't
do you any good," Lena said. "You've got to do
something."

"What can we do?" Willa asked.

"I don't know." Lena paused. "But I do know is

that it's a mystery," she said, her words drawn out to sound spooky. "No, seriously. We should get to the bottom of it. First off, who are our suspects?"

Sarah and Willa glanced at each other.

"This isn't one of your mystery books, Lena. There *aren't* any suspects," Sarah protested. "Buttercup is probably just sick."

"But we don't know for sure," Lena insisted.

"Jasper!" Willa had no idea why she had yelled that name. Sarah glared at her.

"What?" Willa tried to defend herself. "He doesn't want to lose the bet."

"Sarah, you are the one who said how much he likes to win bets," Lena reminded her friend. "That is a motive."

Sarah's shoulders rose as she took a deep breath. "I guess so."

"Great," Lena said. "That's one."

Willa didn't think it was great at all. A horse was sick, and they were accusing someone of poisoning that horse. It seemed horrible!

"We need more suspects." Lena narrowed her eyes, thinking. "What about your dad, Sarah?"

"Lena!" Sarah yelled. "Stop it. This isn't a game. My dad would never do that." She stared at the ground.

"Are you okay?" Willa asked.

"I'm fine, but can we please talk about something else?" She pushed her thick hair behind her ear. She refused to look at Lena.

"Whatever you want," Lena replied with a shrug. "But you won't solve a case by ignoring it."

Willa stared at Lena. She was using all these real detective words. Did she think she was a *real* detective?

Lena started to leave. When she was halfway across the yard, she turned around and walked backward. She pointed at Sarah with both hands. "You know what you need?" she asked excitedly. "A *stakeout*. That way, you'll know if someone is coming by and poisoning Buttercup. And you'll catch him red-handed!"

Willa's eyes grew wide. She couldn't believe Lena! She shook her head and turned to Sarah as Lena walked away.

Sarah tilted her head to one side. Then she titled it to the other. Finally she said to Willa, "A stakeout is not a bad idea. We should do it. Tonight."

Chapter 7

SARAH INSISTED THAT THEY HAVE THE STAKE-out that night. The Summer Extravaganza was only a week away, so there wasn't a lot of time. Even though the stakeout had been Lena's idea, Sarah and Willa were not sure they should invite her.

"She's not always like that," Sarah said. "Maybe it's because we gave her all those books."

"Maybe."

"She's probably been reading those mysteries nonstop since the party," said Sarah. "And this isn't the first time she's done this. She's insisted that something was a *real* mystery before."

After she had given it some thought, Willa decided Lena should join them. It was kind of cool, the way Lena could think like a detective. Willa just didn't want her to upset Sarah.

"We can make it fun. With a tent, sleeping bags, and flashlights," Sarah said. "Mom will make us invite the boys, but we won't tell them it's a stakeout."

Willa agreed that was a good idea. Otherwise, Ben would bring his binoculars, his walkie-talkie with all the beeping buttons, and the long-range water shooter he got for his birthday. They would never get any detective work done! The more she thought about it, the more excited Willa was for that night.

"We can set up the tent here," Sarah said, standing with her arms stretched out. "It's close to the field but not too close. I'll get the tent. Will you ask my mom if you can call Lena?"

Willa went into the house in search of Mrs. Starling. She found her at the kitchen table with a computer and several dictionaries. Mrs. Starling was a book translator.

When Willa called and talked to Lena, she did not mention the stakeout. "Just tell her it's a sleepover," Sarah had said.

But Lena knew the truth at once. "A stakeout is the right thing to do," she said. "I'll bring the marshmallows."

"Great," was Willa's only reply.

Mrs. Starling smiled when Willa handed back the phone. She paused her typing for a moment and adjusted her blue-rimmed glasses. "I used to love outdoor sleepovers," she said. "I wish I weren't so busy, I'd sleep out with you."

"Maybe next time," Willa suggested. Willa really liked Mrs. Starling. With all the kids and animals, the Starlings' house always seemed so fun and lively.

"I'd like that. I hope Bess isn't giving you too much trouble out there." Mrs. Starling mentioned her youngest daughter as she went back to her typing. "You kids are such a help with her."

Willa gave a quick, nervous smile and rushed outside. Where *was* little Bess? She had to find Sarah. "Sarah!" she called. "Sarah?" she repeated when her friend didn't answer.

Sarah came out of the garage. "What?"

"Do you know where Bess is?" Willa asked.

Sarah's eyes immediately filled with worry. "She must be with the boys. They're out back."

They raced to the other side of the house to find Ben and Chipper playing fetch with the puppies. Ben was flat on the ground, being licked by three puppies at once.

"Where's Bess?"

Chipper's face was blank. "I thought she was with *you*."

Willa's heart began to pound.

"No, she's not," Sarah said. "And she's not

with Mom." She looked around the yard. "You guys go down to the dock. Willa will check the fields. I'll look along the street. Now go!"

Everyone ran off. Willa's mind raced in time with her legs. She hadn't even thought about the dock. The very back of the Starlings' yard went down to the bay. It was the stretch of water between Chincoteague and Assateague. She hoped little Bess would not have gone to the water alone.

Willa forced her mind back to the pasture and the fields. If she didn't find Bess there, she'd go to the barn. Her breath was short when she stopped by the pasture fence. She grabbed hold of one of the wooden posts and climbed up for a better view. The pasture had

a trough,

two horses,

one puppy named Amos,

and a lot of grass and bitter yellow flowers.

No Bess.

"Bess!" Willa called. She turned to the field. At first she didn't see anything. Then she noticed something stirring in the waist-high grass. "Bess!" she cried, and ran. Bess was sitting deep in a patch of red clover.

"Sarah! Sarah! I found her!"

After a moment Bess held up a bundle of flowers. "For Buttercup," she announced. "A snack."

Willa smiled and nodded. "Horses love that sweet clover, don't they?" she said, kneeling down. She didn't hear Sarah approach.

"Willa? Bess? Where are you guys?" Sarah pleaded. Willa stood up and waved.

At once Sarah plunged into the tall grass, grabbed Bess under the arms, and lifted the small girl to her hip. "We were so worried," she said.

"She was picking a snack for Buttercup," Willa explained.

"Bess, you can't do that. You can't run off. And you can't feed Buttercup. The vet said no extra food until Buttercup gets better." Sarah brushed the pollen off her sister's pink cheek and squeezed her small body close.

It already felt like a long day, so Willa was sure her parents would say no to the sleepover. Willa and Ben had not been home much in the past week, other than to do their chores. They had spent a lot of time with the Starlings and with Starbuck.

"A sleepover? That sounds great!" Mom exclaimed. "Are you sure the Starlings don't mind?"

"Not at all," Willa answered, stealing a pinch of shredded cheese from the counter. "Mr. Starling already put up the tent."

"Well, that works out perfectly. It'll give us a chance to clean up," Mom said. She hurried down the hallway and opened the closet. It was full of all kinds of tools and supplies. "The carpenters finished their work on the fence and deck today. I want to paint, and it's better if you and your sticky fingers aren't around."

Willa grinned. For once, being messy paid off.

Chapter 8

"YOUR DAD MAKES GOOD CHILI, WILLA," LENA said. It was later that evening. The sleepover had begun, but the sleeping had not. Lena leaned back into one of the beanbag chairs the girls had dragged out from Sarah's house just before the sun set.

The girls were each eating a cup of Willa's dad's soup, and Ben and Chipper were off in the dark, searching for fireflies.

"Thanks. He'd be happy to hear you say that," Willa said, blowing on the lumpy red beans on her spoon. "My family is sick of testing chili. We've tried, like, a dozen recipes over the past two weeks. After we eat, my dad always quizzes us. He expects us to know if he's put in one tablespoon of cumin or two. He really wants to win the chili cook-off at the carnival, but he's driving us crazy!"

"That *is* crazy," Lena agreed, waving her spoon in the air. "My dad always makes the exact same recipe every time."

"And he always wins the Greater Chincoteague Chili Cook-Off," Sarah added. "*Every* time."

Willa's eyebrows shot up.

"Yeah," Lena admitted. "But I really like your dad's. It tastes like there's extra oregano."

Willa's eyebrows shot up even further. Her dad had said something about oregano when she'd tasted the chili earlier that day. Could

Lena really taste that? Maybe she did have superdetective skills after all!

"My mom keeps warning my dad that he shouldn't do anything too fancy," Willa said. "She said that people on the island like their traditions."

"They do!" Sarah agreed. "And there's something special about always having Mr. Wise's chili at the Summer Extravaganza. It just tastes right."

"Well, my dad includes a special ingredient," Lena admitted. "It's a secret."

A secret ingredient? Willa frowned. Her dad had his work cut out for him.

"So," Lena whispered, moving in closer, "the boys don't know this is a stakeout?"

"It's just a sleepover," Sarah insisted.

"Yeah, right," Lena said. "And the Triple Fudge Caramel Brownie Surprise is just another bowl of ice cream." Lena paused to take a bite of corn bread. "You are worried about Buttercup, *and* you want to win that bet. Those are two good reasons for a stakeout." She took another bite. "Don't worry. I will be discreet, and I can stay up late."

Willa smirked. Her friends back in Chicago never used words like *discreet*. It *was* the perfect word to say that she could keep a secret and wouldn't make a big deal about it. Lena knew how to say what she meant. Willa admired that.

Sarah sighed. "All right. We should keep an eye out. I want to find out what's going on, but I hope I can keep my eyes open."

♥

The three girls were quiet for a while. They could hear the boys running after the fire-flies, whooping every time they caught or missed one.

"If they aren't quiet, they'll scare away all the suspects," Lena mumbled.

Willa didn't want to believe there were any *real* suspects. Why would anyone want to poison Buttercup?

They ate super-gooey s'mores with peanut-butter cups melted inside. They counted bats swooping through the sky. They wondered who their teacher would be in the fall.

But they didn't see anything suspicious.

When it was time for bed, the boys joined them. They could all fit in the Starlings' enormous tent—the sleeping bags didn't even touch! Lena held a flashlight to her chin and told a spooky story about a ghost horse, the shadows playing across her face. Even though there was a sick horse in the pasture nearby, no one seemed to mind. The story was *that* good.

Willa couldn't guess how late it was when Mr. Starling made them turn off their flashlights. There were annoying mosquitoes, but Lena insisted they sleep with the tent flaps open. "How else will we see anything?" she asked when Sarah protested.

Early the next morning Willa woke with a foot in her face. Actually, she woke up just *after* a foot had been in her face. "Yuck! Ow! Ben?"

"Sorry," he said as he tripped out of the tent. Chipper followed him.

Willa poked Sarah and then Lena. "Did you see anyone? Did you hear anything? Did you see our suspect?" Willa asked. She propped herself up on her elbows.

"Not a thing. No one came by at all." Lena rubbed her eyes with her fingertips. She sat cross-legged with her pillow in her lap.

"At least no one that we saw," Sarah corrected.

"I told you, I can stay up late," Lena said. "I'm pretty sure no one came by. I would have seen him . . . or her."

Willa took a closer look at Lena. Her eyes

looked red! "You look like you didn't sleep at all."

Lena raised her eyebrows. "That's a good observation."

Had Lena stayed up all night? The detective stood up and started to shove her sleeping bag into its tiny duffel. "I've got to go home."

"But Mom will make pancakes," said Sarah. "Maybe with whipped cream."

"No, thanks," Lena answered. "I don't want pancakes. I just want my own bed."

At the breakfast table Mr. Starling told the girls he had checked on Buttercup that morning, and she was about the same. He shook his head. "She's got the same puffy lips. The same dull eyes."

"The same stinky manure," Chipper added.

"Chipper, we're eating!" scolded Sarah.

"What?" he asked. "Ben's grandma told us to keep an eye on it. We have to make sure it doesn't get too runny."

"It's good that you're helpful, dear," Mrs. Starling said.

Ben nudged Chipper with his elbow, and both boys snorted.

Sarah pulled Willa aside after breakfast. "You know," she began, "there must be some way we can find out if Jasper is behind Buttercup being sick."

"I agree," Willa said, leaning against the family-room wall. "But just so you know, I don't think it's him. I only yelled out his name because Lena was being so pushy."

"Don't worry. She gets like that," Sarah answered.

"Well, what should we do?"

Sarah looked Willa in the eye. "We can ask him."

Why hadn't Willa thought of that?

Chapter 9

WILLA AND SARAH HOPPED ON THEIR BIKES
and headed to the other side of the island. They
hoped Jasper would be around to answer their
questions.

Sarah knocked on the door. Jasper's mom
smiled when she saw her. Sarah introduced
Willa and said they had a question for Jasper.
His mom said he was in the backyard.

"That seemed easy," Willa whispered.

They rounded the corner and immediately saw Jasper—sitting in a kiddie pool, reading comics.

"What are *you* doing here?" he asked, quickly standing up. A trickle of water ran off his swimming trunks. "Trying to get out of our bet?" He sounded pretty sure of himself.

"Maybe you wanted to get a look at Wrangler. He's in the barn."

"Not really," Sarah said. "I actually have a question for you. It's kind of weird." Sarah went on to explain how sick Buttercup was. It took a while, but Jasper's jaw dropped when he realized what Sarah was hinting at.

"That's horrible!" he exclaimed. "I would never do that to a horse. I mean, it's just a bet. It's just a bowl of ice cream."

A picture of the extra-large scoops topped with a brownie and caramel flashed in Willa's head. It wasn't just *any* bowl of ice cream, but she totally believed Jasper. By the look on his face, he would never do anything to hurt a horse.

"That's what I thought," Sarah said, shoving

her hands in her pockets. "We just had to make sure. We're following all our leads."

Willa almost laughed, but Jasper looked serious. "I'm sorry your horse is sick. I'll let you know if I think of anything." He pressed his lips together. "I'll let you out of the bet if you want."

"No." Sarah shook her head. "A bet's a bet."

They said good-bye and headed back to their bikes. "'We're following all our leads'?" Willa said to her friend. "That's real detective talk. I'll have to tell Lena."

Sarah squealed. "Don't you dare!"

Willa laughed. It was a relief that Jasper was no longer a suspect, but they still didn't know what was wrong with Buttercup. And the carnival was less than a week away.

♥

Willa checked in with Sarah every day. Her friend had given up hope of being part of the parade. Buttercup was the same—no better, no worse. All week, both Willa and Ben helped out as much as they could, at home and at Miller Farm. They both had a chance to ride Starbuck again, with Grandma watching as closely as always. Their favorite pony was definitely healthy again.

One afternoon Grandma Edna offered them a ride on the beach as a special thank-you for all their help. Ben sat on Jake, the big draft horse. Grandma even let him take the reins. "Don't you worry," she said, patting Ben on the leg. "Jake likes to stay close to the others. He won't wander off." Ben sat tall in the saddle. He was twice his normal height!

Willa was just as pleased when Grandma

gave her permission to ride Starbuck. "Really?" she said.

"Well, why wouldn't I let you ride her? You two get along so well." Grandma Edna smoothed her hand along Starbuck's toffee-colored neck. "You're just about the steadiest mare ever, aren't you? I wouldn't trust just any pony with my granddaughter."

Willa wondered if she should tell Grandma that she wanted to ride in the parade, that she wanted to ride in the parade on Starbuck! But Willa decided not to say anything. For now, getting to ride Starbuck on the beach was more than enough.

Willa's mood was still happy as they rode home on their bikes. "Was it fun on Jake?" she yelled to Ben over her shoulder.

"It was awesome!" Ben declared. "I could see for miles!"

Horseback riding on the beach was always amazing. Willa loved to gaze over at Assateague and think about the wild ponies. It was hard to believe that Starbuck had been born on that tiny island—that she was once part of the sandy shore, the marsh grass, and the sea breeze.

As they approached the Starlings' place, Willa was trying to imagine Starbuck as a foal.

"Hey, look!" Ben called. "There's Bess. She's feeding Buttercup *again*."

Willa blinked and tried to focus. Sure enough, the little girl was right back at the pasture fence. She must have escaped from Sarah's supervision again.

"We have to tell the Starlings," Willa said,

swerving her bike into the gravel driveway. Ben skidded to a stop behind her.

She pushed the doorbell three times, fast. Then she ran toward the pasture.

Ben was just a few steps behind her. Mr. Starling spotted him when he answered the door. "Ben Dunlap, are you playing a trick on me?" he called out. Sarah and Chipper's dad had a jolly tone, until he saw Ben's face.

"It's Bess," Ben yelled. "She's by the pasture, sir."

Willa was already kneeling down next to Bess, making sure she was okay. The little girl had been leaning over the bottom board of the fence, trying to get closer to her favorite horse.

"For Buttercup," Bess said, holding out another bouquet.

"Yes," Willa replied. "You picked clover for Buttercup."

Bess shook her head. *"Buttercups* for Buttercup," she declared.

Willa slowly took in the words. "Can I see?" she asked Bess hopefully.

Bess nodded and handed over the bouquet with pride.

Mr. Starling had arrived, with Ben and Sarah and Chipper close behind.

Willa stood up and held out the bouquet. "I think we might have solved the mystery," she said.

♥

It was hard to believe that Bess had been feeding Buttercup some of the toxic flowers. Willa called Grandma Edna from the Starlings' house to get advice.

"There was just one strand in the whole big bouquet," Willa explained. "When we asked Bess, she said that Buttercup didn't like the buttercup flowers, so she hid them in the clover. Bess wanted Buttercup to eat the buttercups because they had the same name."

Grandma said it was good news that the horse didn't like the taste of the flowers. "Since she wasn't that sick, I'm sure she'll recover. She didn't show any of the serious signs of poisoning. But you have to get the horse away from Bess. We can't have the little girl feeding the horse any more toxic plants."

Grandma had come up with an easy solution: Buttercup should live at Misty Inn for the time being. The workers had fixed the fence. Willa and Ben's mom had painted it. And there was a clean stall in the barn. Grandma called to make sure it was okay, and she promised to come by later to check on the horse. Willa was relieved that they'd solved the problem, but she doubted it was time to help Sarah win the bet. The parade was in just three days.

"We're going to have a horse living in our field? In our barn?" Ben could hardly believe it.

"It's awfully nice of your folks to take Buttercup in," Mr. Starling said as he led the mare out of the pasture.

"Bye-bye, Buttercup," Bess said from her

mother's arms. She sniffed and leaned her head on her mom's shoulder.

"It's okay," Willa said in her kindest voice. "She's not going very far. You can come visit her at our house."

Buttercup swished her tail and took her time on the short journey. Meanwhile, Amos yipped and ran circles around the whole traveling band.

"That puppy seems to have adopted Buttercup," noted Mr. Starling.

"Yeah," Ben said. "He's always sneaking into the pasture to see her. They're friends."

"It's not as odd as you might think," Mr. Starling said. "I'm afraid you might be getting more than one new animal as guests at your inn."

Willa locked eyes with Ben. Was Mr. Starling

saying what she thought he was saying? Willa crossed her fingers. It was great, knowing that they could offer Buttercup a safe, happy home, but if getting Amos was part of the deal, that would be even better.

Chapter 10

GRANDMA EDNA HAD BEEN RIGHT. THE SOLU-
tion was easy. Buttercup started to improve as
soon as she was at Misty Inn. The very next
day, she was playfully nipping at Amos again.
Willa and Ben volunteered to look after the
sweet chestnut horse. Taking care of her was
too fun to seem like a chore!

Willa couldn't believe it, but even her parents

agreed it was nice to have a horse in their field. "It feels right," Mom said on Friday morning as she looked out the kitchen window.

"Mmm-hmm," Dad murmured from behind the stove, where the final pot of chili was brewing. The carnival was the next day, and Dad wanted his chosen recipe's flavors "to blend and deepen overnight." Whatever that meant.

Willa and Ben thought it was funny that no one ever talked about how, in the process of taking in Buttercup, they had also adopted a puppy—a feisty, funny puppy who was happy to race in the field and sleep in the barn.

What everyone did want to talk about was the parade. Mr. Starling decided *not* to ride Buttercup. He wanted to give her time to recover. He did, however, agree to let Sarah ride Sweetums. "This way, I can walk right by your side," he told his daughter. "The parade can get kind of crazy."

Grandma Edna had said the exact same thing, and she had meant it. But she had been so impressed with how Willa and Ben had helped around the farm and cared for the ailing Buttercup, she was willing to make an exception. She told her grandkids they could ride in the parade too. Willa would be on Starbuck and Ben on Jake, and she would walk with them, just to be safe.

On the morning of parade day, Mom dropped the kids off at Miller Farm. They planned to put on their costumes in the barn and ride down to

Main Street. There, they would meet up with Sarah and her dad.

"We'll be watching for you near the carnival grounds," Mom reminded them. "Be careful and have fun!"

"Be careful and have fun" seemed like the slogan for the parade. It was what all the adults said to them, but Willa and Ben were not worried. First of all, Grandma Edna would be there. Second of all, Willa trusted Starbuck and Ben trusted Jake. They had both spent a lot of time with the horses to make sure the animals trusted them, too.

As they marched toward Main Street, Willa could not stop smiling. She was dressed like Annie Oakley, the famous sharpshooter from the Old West. Starbuck even looked a little like Annie's horse on the TV show. Ben was dressed like a Jedi Knight, with a long brown robe that covered his whole backside and most of Jake's, too.

Grandma made *tsk-tsk* sounds when she saw the crowd in front of the hardware store. "If you told me this time last year that I'd be leading my two grandkids in this mess, I never would have believed you," she said. Willa wor-

ried that Grandma might just turn them back around. Grandma was stubborn, but she was also a woman of her word. "I see Lloyd Starling over there. Let's go."

Sarah looked almost magical in her Glinda the Good Witch costume. She was excited to see Willa and Ben, but she was almost more excited to see Jasper Langely.

"Hey, Jasper," she called out. "Guess who owes me a Triple Fudge Caramel Brownie Surprise?"

Jasper tapped his finger to his chest. "Me," he said.

"Is that Wrangler?" Willa asked, looking at the horse Jasper was riding.

"No," he admitted. "My dad decided to ride Wrangler at the last second. This is Snacktime."

Willa nodded. The bay horse had long whiskers on her chin and a full round belly. "I like her name," Willa said genuinely. "It fits her."

"You're telling me," Jasper said, and he patted the horse's tummy. "She could eat two of those sundaes, no problem."

The local drum corps and brass band signaled the start of the parade with the song

"Seventy-Six Trombones." Ben could feel the beat of the drums in his chest. He sat tall on Jake's back. Willa gave Starbuck a reassuring pat and wrapped her fingers in the pony's coal-black mane.

The parade made its way right through the center of town. Both neighbors and strangers lined the streets, cheering and waving as the horses passed. Bunches of colorful balloons bobbed in the air, marking the parade path. Willa saw clowns, teenagers on stilts, and some women in long skirts on old-fashioned bicycles, but the ponies and horses were the real stars of the show.

As they neared the carnival grounds, Ben and Willa spotted their parents. Mom waved as Dad took pictures. Grandpa Reed was there.

Lena, Chipper, and the rest of the Starlings yelled from the crowd too.

Once they reached the end of the parade route, Grandma took Starbuck's and Jake's reins. "These two have done their job for the day," she said, feeding each an apple slice. "I'll take them home and then come back. You kids have fun. You've earned it."

Willa threw her arms around her grandma. "Thank you," she said into the sleeve of Grandma's jean jacket. "Thank you so much. This has been the best day I've had since we moved."

Grandma Edna put her hand on Willa's head. "Of course, dear."

"Thanks, Grandma," Ben said as he handed her his helmet. "It was fun."

Willa looked at her brother and rolled her eyes. "It was more than fun," she said. "It was *the best*." She gave Starbuck a kiss, and they went off to find their friends.

After cotton candy, corn on the cob, and lemonade, they hardly had any room for chili. But they still went to the Greater Chincoteague Chili Cook-off booth.

Even though there were ten different chilis, Willa knew which one was her dad's. So did Lena. "It's the recipe with extra oregano," Lena said. "It was a good choice. I voted for him to win."

Willa did too.

When the winner of the chili contest announcement was made, the crowd wasn't surprised that Lena's father managed to win again.

"It's okay, Dad," Willa said as Mom pinned the red second-place ribbon on Dad's T-shirt. "Lena said Mr. Wise has a secret ingredient, and he uses it every year."

Dad sighed. "I figured as much," he said. "It tasted a little bit like chocolate. Maybe next year I should compete in the chowder cook-off instead."

Now Mom sighed and laughed. "At least we have a year to prepare," she said.

"Willa, Ben, come on!" The Dunlap kids looked up to see their friends pointing toward the Ferris wheel.

Willa, Sarah, and Lena sat together. Chipper and Ben were in the car just below. Willa drew in a deep breath, and she could smell the carnival: the horses, the chili, the funnel cakes, the salt from the ocean.

Once they were near the top, she could see all the way to their house. Buttercup was grazing in the field! She couldn't see New Cat or Amos, but she knew they were there, just as she knew the wild horses were over on Assateague.

It felt good. She reached out and took one of Sarah's and one of Lena's hands in hers. Willa was starting to believe her family belonged on the island, and their house was starting to be a real home—filled with people and animals that she loved. They really did feel like Chincoteague kids now.

ABOUT THE SERIES

Marguerite Henry's Misty Inn series is inspired by the award-winning books by Marguerite Henry, the beloved author of such classic horse stories as *King of the Wind*; *Misty of Chincoteague*; *Justin Morgan Had a Horse*; *Stormy, Misty's Foal*; *Misty's Twilight*, and *Album of Horses*, among many other titles.

Learn more about the world of Marguerite Henry at www.MistyofChincoteague.com.